The Wind in the Willows

The River Bank

Illustrated by Val Biro

Macdonald Purnell

ISBN 0 361 06338 5
Copyright © 1984 Purnell Publishers Limited
Published 1984 by Purnell Books
a division of Macdonald & Co (Publishers) Ltd
Maxwell House, 74 Worship Street, London EC2A 2EN
Reprinted 1986
Made and printed in Great Britain by
Purnell and Sons (Book Production) Limited
Member of the BPCC Group

The Mole had been working very hard all morning, spring-cleaning his little home. He had dust in his throat and eyes, and splashes of whitewash all over his black fur. His back was aching and his arms were weary.

The Wind in the Willows

The River Bank

PURNELL

Suddenly he flung down his brush on the floor. "Bother!" he said, and "O blow," and also "Hang spring-cleaning." Then he bolted out of the house without even waiting to put on his coat.

He made for a steep little tunnel outside.
"Up we go!" he said as he scraped and
scrabbled, working busily with his little
paws. At last, pop! his snout came out into

the sunlight, and he found himself rolling in
the warm grass of a great meadow.

"This is better than whitewashing!" he
said to himself. In the delight of spring
without its cleaning he rambled hither and
thither through the meadows. And instead of

having an uneasy conscience pricking him
and whispering "whitewash!" he could only
feel how jolly it was to be idle.

Suddenly he came to a river. Never in his

life had he seen a river before. All was a-shake and a-shiver—glints and gleams and sparkles, rustle and swirl, chatter and bubble. Mole was fascinated.

A dark hole in the bank opposite, just above the water's edge, caught his eye. As he gazed, something bright and small seemed to twinkle in the heart of it. Then, as he looked, it winked at him. It was an eye.

A little brown face with whiskers gradually appeared. Small neat ears and thick silky hair.

It was the Water Rat!

The two animals stood and regarded each other curiously.

"Hullo, Mole!" said the Water Rat.

"Hullo, Rat!" said the Mole.

"Would you like to come over?" enquired the Rat presently. He stepped into a little boat, sculled smartly across and made fast.

Then the Rat held up his fore-paw as the Mole stepped gingerly down. "Lean on that!" he said. "Now then, step lively!" And Mole, to his surprise and delight, found himself actually seated in the stern of a real boat.

"This has been a wonderful day!" said he as the Rat shoved off. "Do you know, I've never been in a boat before in all my life."

"What?" cried the Rat, open-mouthed. "What have you been doing, then?"

"Is it as nice as all that?" asked Mole shyly.

"Nice? It's the *only* thing," said the Water Rat solemnly as he began to row. "Believe me, my young friend, there is *nothing* half so much worth doing as simply messing about in boats.

"Simply messing," he went on dreamily, "messing—about—in boats—"

"Look ahead, Rat!" cried the Mole suddenly.

It was too late. The boat struck the bank full tilt and Rat lay on his back at the bottom of the boat.

He picked himself up with a pleasant laugh. "Look here! If you've really nothing else to do this morning, supposing we go down the river together, and have a day of it?"

The Mole waggled his toes from sheer happiness. "What a day I'm having. Let us

start at once!" he said.

"Hold on a minute, then," said the Rat. He tied the boat to the landing stage and climbed back into his hole above. Shortly he reappeared with a fat, wicker luncheon basket.

"Shove that under your feet," he said to

the Mole. Then he untied the boat and took the sculls again.

Mole trailed a paw in the water while the Water Rat sculled on steadily.

"What lies over there?" Mole asked, waving a paw.

"That? O, that's just the Wild Wood," answered the Rat. "We don't go there much,

we river-bankers."

"And beyond the Wild Wood?" Mole asked.

"Beyond the Wild Wood comes the Wide World," said the Rat. "I've never been there

and I'm never going. Nor you either if you've got any sense at all. Now then! Here's our backwater at last, where we're going to lunch."

The Rat brought the boat alongside the bank and made her fast. He helped the still awkward Mole safely ashore and swung out the luncheon basket.

His excited friend shook out the table-cloth and spread it. Then he took out all the mysterious packets one by one.

"O my! O my!" he exclaimed at each in turn.

When all was ready, Rat said, "Now pitch in, old fellow."

From where they sat they could get a glimpse of the main stream across the island that separated them. Just then another boat flashed into view. The rower, a short stout Toad, splashed badly and rolled a good deal.

"He'll be out of that boat in a minute if he rolls like that," said the Rat. "Well, well, I suppose we ought to be moving. I wonder which of us ought to pack the luncheon basket."

"O, please, let me," said the Mole. So of course Rat let him. Packing the basket was not quite such pleasant work as unpacking it.

The afternoon sun was getting low as the Rat sculled gently homewards. Already Mole

was quite at home in a boat (so he thought).
He was getting a bit restless and presently he
said, "Ratty! Please, *I* want to row now!"

The Rat shook his head with a smile. "Not
yet, my young friend," he said. "Wait till

you've had a few lessons. It's not as easy as it looks.''

The Mole was quiet for a minute or two. He began to feel jealous of Rat. His pride began to whisper that he could do it every bit as well.

Suddenly, he jumped up and seized the sculls. Rat was taken by surprise and fell backwards off his seat.

"Stop it, you *silly* ass!" cried the Rat, from the bottom of the boat.

The Mole made a great dig at the water.
He missed the surface altogether, his legs
flew up above his head. The next moment—
Sploosh!

Over went the boat and he found himself

struggling in the river.

O my, how cold the water was. How it sang in his ears as he went down, down! Then a firm paw gripped him by the back of his neck. It was the Rat.

Laughing, Rat propelled the helpless animal ashore. Then he hauled him on to the bank. Mole was a squashy lump of misery.

The Rat rubbed him down a bit and wrung some of the wet out of him. "Now," he said, "trot up and down until you're warm and dry again, while I dive for the luncheon basket."

When all was ready to start once more the Mole took his place in the boat. In a low voice he said, "Ratty, I'm very sorry. My heart fails me when I think how I might have lost that beautiful luncheon basket. I have been a complete ass. Will you forgive me?"

"That's all right, bless you!" responded the Rat cheerily. "What's a little wet to a Water Rat? I'm more in the water than out of it most days.

"Look here, I really think you had better stop with me for a little time. It's very plain and rough. Not like Toad's fine house—but you haven't seen that yet. Still, I can make you comfortable. And I'll teach you to row, and to swim."

The Mole was so touched by his kind manner of speaking that he could find no voice to answer him.

When they got home the Rat made a bright fire in the parlour and planted Mole in an

armchair in front of it. He told him river
stories until supper-time.

Supper was a most cheerful meal. Shortly afterwards a terribly sleepy Mole had to be escorted upstairs to the best bedroom. He

laid his head on the pillow in great peace and
contentment.

This day was only the first of many similar ones for Mole. Each of them was longer and full of interest as the ripening summer moved onwards. He learned to swim and to row. And with his ear to the reed stems he could sometimes catch what the wind whispered among them.